First German

AT SCHOOL

Kathy Gemmell and Jenny Tyler
Illustrated by Sue Stitt
Designed by Diane Thistlethwaite

Consultant: Sandy Walker

CONTENTS

First published in 1993 by Usborne Publishing Ltd.
Usborne House, 83-85 Saffron Hill
London EC1N 8RT, England.
Copyright © 1993 Usborne Publishing Ltd.
Printed in Portugal. UE

First published in America March 1994

Speaking German

This book is about the Strudel [shtroodel] family. They are going to help you learn to speak German.

Word lists

You will find a word list on every double page to tell you what the German words mean.

Guten Tag
gootn tahg

Word list

Guten Tag gootn tahg	hello
Hallo hullaw	hi
ich heiße ikh hyssa	I am called
Onkel onkel	uncle
Entschuldigung entshooldigoong	sorry
du bist dran doo bist dran	your turn
wo ist die Katze? vaw ist dee katsa	where is the cat?

Hallo
hullaw

The little letters are to help you say the German words. Read them as if they were English words.

Ich heiße
ikh hyssa
Markus.
mahrkoos

Ich heiße
ikh hyssa
Onkel Helmut.
onkel helmoot

Wo ist
vaw ist
die Katze?
dee katsa

Entschuldigung
entshooldigoong

The best way to find out how to say German words is to listen to a German person speaking. Some letters and sounds are a bit different from English. Here are some clues to help you.

When you see a "ch" in German, it is written "kh" in the little letters. Say this like the "h" in "huge". Say *ich* [ikh], which means "I". Some "ch"s are more like the "ch" in the Scottish word "loch".

Say "sch" like the "sh" in "show".

When you see one of these:ß, just say it like a double "s".

The "ei" in German sounds like "eye". Try saying *ich heiße* [ikh hyssa] which means "I am called".

The letter "j" in German sounds like the English "y".

Try saying out loud what each person on this page is saying.

See if you can find Josefina the mouse on each double page.

Games with word lists

You can play games with the word lists if you like. Here are some ideas.

1. Cover all the English words and see if you can say the English for each German word. Score a point for each one you can remember.

2. Time yourself and see if you can say the whole list more quickly next time.

3. Race a friend. The first one to say the English for each word scores a point. The winner is the one to score the most points.

4. Play all these games the other way around, saying the German for each English word.

Du bist dran
Look for the *du bist dran* [doo bist dran] boxes in this book. There is something for you to do in each of them. *Du bist dran* means "your turn".

Look out for the joke bubbles on some of the pages.

3

In the classroom

Silvia and Markus Strudel are back at school today. There is a new boy in their class. He introduces himself by saying *Ich heiße Jörg* [ikh hyssa yerg]. *Ich heiße* is how you say "I am called" or "my name is" in German.

Can you help the children introduce themselves to Jörg, by saying what's in each speech bubble? Use the word list to help you.

Can you work out which way Jörg should go so that he only passes each of them once and ends up at the teacher's desk?

Names

Strudel shtroodel	**Uli** oolee
Ziffer tsiffer	**Jörg** yerg
Rainer ryner	**Anke** unka
Silvia zilveeya	**Petra** paytra
Markus mahrkoos	**Klaus** klaowss
Katja katya	**Rudi** roody

Word list

wie heißt du? vee hyste doo	what's your name?
ich heiße ikh hyssa	I am called/my name is
er heißt air hyste	he is called
sie heißt zee hyste	she is called
meine Mutter myna rnootter	my mother
mein Vater myne fahter	my father
mein Bruder mine brooder	my brother
meine Schwester myna shvester	my sister
Herr hair	Mr.
Frau fraow	Mrs.
Oma awma	Granny

4

Ich heiße Silvia.

Ich heiße Markus.

Ich heiße Rudi.

Ich heiße Klaus.

Ich heiße Anke.

Happy families

Can you match up the people in the column on the right with the person who is talking about them? Use the word list see what all the words mean.

Meine Mutter heißt Oma Strudel.

Ich heiße Rainer.

Mein Vater heißt Herr Strudel.

Ich heiße Oma Strudel.

Mein Bruder heißt Rainer.

Ich heiße Silvia.

Meine Schwester heißt Silvia.

Ich heiße Herr Strudel.

What is Markus's sister called?
What is Silvia's father called?
Can you answer in German? *Er heißt* [air hyste] means "he is called" and *sie heißt* [zee hyste] means "she is called".

Du bist dran
Wie heißt du? [vee hyste doo].
What's your name? Try and introduce yourself and your family in German, using the words on this page to help you.

How are you?

Look at the picture to see how everyone is this morning.

To ask how someone is in German you say *Wie geht's?* [vee gates] which means, "How are you?"

Frau Ziffer is talking to someone who is saying "I'm very well, thank you," in German. Use the word list to see how to say this out loud.

Where are they?

Can you spot the following people in the picture?

Someone who has toothache?

Someone with a headache?

Someone who is saying "My leg hurts"?

Someone with a tummy-ache?

Someone who feels all right?

Use the word list to help you say out loud in German what each person is saying.

Can you spot the words for arm, leg, hand and foot on this page?

der Arm
dair arm

der Fuß
dair fooss

das Bein
dass bine

At home

Here are some of the Strudel family at home. They should be saying how they feel but the speech bubbles have all been mixed up. Can you say what each person should be saying?

6

Word list

Guten Tag *gootn tahg*	good morning, hello
danke *dunka*	thank you
wie geht's? *vee gates*	how are you?
(es geht mir) sehr gut *ess gate meer zair goot*	I'm very well
ich habe Zahnweh *ikh hahba tsahnvay*	I have toothache
ich habe Kopfweh *ikh hahba kopfvay*	I have a headache
ich habe Bauchweh *ikh hahba baowkhvay*	I have a tummy-ache
mein Bein tut mir weh *mine bine toot meer vay*	my leg hurts
Oma *awma*	Granny
Frau *fraow*	Mrs.
Herr *hair*	Mr.

Der, die and *das*

Did you notice that some of the words have *der, die* or *das* before them? This means "the" in German.

All naming words (nouns) are masculine, feminine or neuter in German. You use *der* for masculine words, *die* for feminine words and *das* for neuter words. You cannot guess which is which, so you have to learn words with their *der, die* or *das*.

In German, all nouns begin with a capital letter.

Du bist dran
Wie geht's? [vee gates].

How do you feel at the moment? Look at what everyone in the cloakroom is saying to help you say how you feel today. Ask your family and friends how they are in German. You could draw pictures of them and give them German speech bubbles.

Counting

Can you help Silvia with her counting? Look at the first picture to see her counting the books. Count the things in the other pictures in the same way, starting with *eins* [ine ts], *zwei* [tsvy].

How many things are in each picture? Answer by saying *es gibt* [ess gipt] and then the number of things you have counted. Use the word list to see how to say all the words.

Number list

eins ine ts	one	**fünf** foonf	five	**acht** akht	eight
zwei tsvy	two	**sechs** zex	six	**neun** noyn	nine
drei dry	three	**sieben** zeebn	seven	**zehn** tsain	ten
vier feer	four				

Word list

es gibt ess gipt	there is, there are
die Geschenke dee geshenka	presents
die Bleistifte dee bly shtifta	pencils
die Regenschirme dee raygn sheerma	umbrellas
die Bücher dee boosher	books
die Hüte dee hoota	hats
die Pflanzen dee pfluntsn	plants

Die means "the" when you are talking about more than one object (plural). You don't say *die* after a number.

Du bist dran

Look for things around your house to count. Count them in German. If you want to continue past ten, here are the numbers up to twenty:

elf elf	eleven	**sechzehn** zekh tsain	sixteen
zwölf tsverlf	twelve	**siebzehn** zeep tsain	seventeen
dreizehn dry tsain	thirteen	**achtzehn** akht tsain	eighteen
vierzehn feer tsain	fourteen	**neunzehn** noyn tsain	nineteen
fünfzehn foonf tsain	fifteen	**zwanzig** tsvan tsikh	twenty

Eins, zwei, drei, vier, fünf, sechs, sieben, acht, neun, zehn.

Es gibt zehn Bücher.

Bücher

Pflanzen

Regenschirme

Geschenke

Bleistifte

Hüte

Song

Here are the first three verses of a German song. Can you sing it right up to *Zehn Hund' wollten spiel'n...* using all the numbers up to ten in German? Sing it to the tune of "One man went to mow". You can see the tune on page 32 if you don't know it.

Ein Hund wollte spiel'n, wollte Fußball spielen,
ine hoont vollta shpeeln vollta foossbal shpeelen
Ein Hund und sein Herr wollten Fußball spielen.
ine hoont oont zine hair vollten foossbal shpeelen

Zwei Hund' wollten spiel'n, wollten
tsvy hoont vollten shpeeln vollten
 Fußball spielen,
 foossbal shpeelen
Zwei Hund', ein Hund und sein Herr wollten
tsvy hoont ine hoont oont zine hair vollten
 Fußball spielen.
 foossbal shpeelen

Drei Hund' wollten spiel'n, wollten
dry hoont vollten shpeeln vollten
 Fußball spielen,
 foossbal shpeelen
Drei Hund', zwei Hund', ein Hund und sein Herr
dry hoont tsvy hoont ine hoont oont zine hair
 wollten Fußball spielen.
 vollten foossbal shpeelen

Here is what the song means in English:

One dog wanted to play, wanted to play football,
One dog and his master wanted to play football.
Two dogs wanted to play ... etc.

Was ergibt sich, wenn
vass airgipt zikh ven
man einen Elefanten mit
mun ine n ellay funten mit
einem Känguruh kreuzt?
ine m kengooroo kroytst

Ganz große
gants grawssa
Löcher überall in
lersher ooberull in
Australien.
owsstrahlian

9

Joke: What do you get if you cross an elephant with a kangaroo?
Great big holes all over Australia.

Days of the week

Silvia and Markus both have timetables to tell them which subject their group will be doing each day.

Using Silvia and Markus's timetables, can you see which day it is in each of the pictures? Say *es ist* [ess ist] which means "it is" and then the day of the week. Look at the word list to see how to say each of the days.

Silvia	
Montag	Zeichnen
Dienstag	Deutsch
Mittwoch	Sport
Donnerstag	Englisch
Freitag	Musik
Samstag	das
Sonntag	Wochenende

Markus	
Montag	Sport
Dienstag	Zeichnen
Mittwoch	Englisch
Donnerstag	Deutsch
Freitag	Musik
Samstag	das
Sonntag	Wochenende

Word list

es ist ess ist	it is
Montag mawntahg	Monday
Dienstag deenstahg	Tuesday
Mittwoch mitvokh	Wednesday
Donnerstag donnerstahg	Thursday
Freitag frytahg	Friday
Samstag zamstahg	Saturday
Sonntag zonntag	Sunday
das Wochenende dass vokhen enda	weekend
Deutsch doytch	German
Englisch eng glish	English
Sport shport	sport
Zeichnen tsykhnen	drawing, art
Musik moozeek	music
heute hoyta	today

How many times can you spot the word *das* on these two pages? Remember, *das* is how you say "the" when you are talking about neuter words. For masculine words, "the" is *der* and for feminine words "the" is *die*.

Indoor hopscotch

Hopscotch in German is called *Himmel-und-Hölle* [himmel oont herla]. Here is a type of hopscotch you can play indoors.

Using the word list to help you, write out the days of the week in German on seven squares of paper (each one large enough to put your foot on).

The aim of the game is to collect as many of the paper squares as possible.

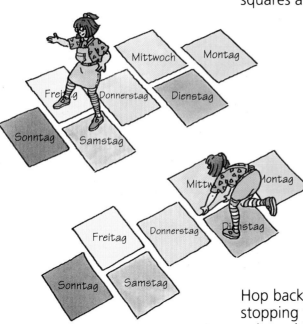

Arrange the seven squares on the floor like this with *Montag* (Monday) nearest you:

Stand about 1m (3ft) away from the first square. Throw a coin onto any one of the squares. Say that day out loud in German, using *es ist* and then the day. (If the stone lands between or outside the squares, throw again.)

Then hop up the squares, putting one foot on each of the squares that are side by side, without stepping on the square with the stone on it. You can only hop once on the top square (*Sonntag*).

Hop back to the beginning, stopping to pick up the coin and its paper square on the way.

Continue until you have thrown the coin onto all the squares. Remember to say each of the days out loud in German. You will have to hop over wider and wider gaps as you pick up more and more squares.

You can play this game by yourself, or with a friend. If you are playing with a friend, take turns to throw. The winner is the one with the most paper squares at the end.

Joke: Waiter, there's a spider in my soup!
I'm sorry, sir, it's the fly's day off.

Du bist dran
Can you say in German what day it is today? "Today" in German is *heute* [hoyta]. Say *es ist heute* [ess ist hoyta] then the day. Try saying what day it is in German every morning for a week.

11

Putting on a play

Everyone is getting ready for the school play. Most of the children seem to have lost something in the piles of clothes lying around the stage.

To say, "I have lost," in German, you say *ich habe* [ikh hahba], then what you have lost and then you say *verloren* [fair lawren].

So to say, "I have lost my watch," you would say *Ich habe meine Armbanduhr verloren* [ikh hahba myna armbandoor fair lawren].

Using the word list to help you, can you say in German what each child is saying?

Can you find all of the lost objects somewhere in the picture?

Ich habe... ...verloren.

Ich habe... ...verloren.

Ich habe... ...verloren.

Ich habe... ...verloren.

Ich habe... ...verloren.

Ich habe... ...verloren.

Word list

ich habe...verloren	I have lost	..meine Brille..	my glasses
ikh hahba...fair lawren		myna brilla	
..meine Handschuhe..	my gloves	..meinen Bleistift..	my pencil
myna hunt shooa		mynen blyshtift	
..meinen Hut..	my hat	..mein Etui..	my pencil case
mynen hoot		mine aytoo ee	
..meinen Gürtel..	my belt	..meine Filzstifte..	my felt tips
mynen girtle		myna filts shtifta	
..meine Armbanduhr..	my watch	..mein Heft..	my exercise book
myna armbandoor		mine heft	
..meine Strickjacke..	my cardigan	und	and
myna shtrik yukka		oont	

Ich habe...
...verloren.

Du bist dran

Here is a German memory game that you can play with two or more players. One person starts by saying *ich habe* [ikh hahba], then the name of an object in German, then *verloren* [fair lawren]. You can use any of the objects on this page.

Take turns repeating what the person before has said but adding another object to the list each time. You only need to say *verloren* once, at the end of each turn. To say "and " in German, you say *und* [oont]. You are out if you can't remember everything in the right order or can't think of an object to add. The winner is the last one to be out.

Ich habe...
...verloren.

Ich habe
meine Filzstifte
verloren...

Ich habe meine
Filzstifte und
meinen Bleistift
verloren...

Ich habe meine
Filzstifte, meinen
Bleistift und mein
Heft verloren...

Ich habe...
...verloren.

13

Art class

Katja has painted a picture of an animal she particularly likes, using her favourite colour.

Look how she says which colour and animal she likes best.

Can you see which is Katja's painting?

Use the word list to help you match each of Katja's friends with their pictures.

Word list

mein Lieblingstier ist..	my favourite animal is..
mine leeblingsteer ist	
meine Lieblingsfarbe ist..	my favourite colour is..
myna leeblingsfarba ist	
die Katze	the cat
dee katsa	
der Hund	the dog
dair hoont	
das Kaninchen	the rabbit
dass ka neen khn	
die Maus	the mouse
dee mouse	
das Pferd	the horse
dass pfairt	
der Elefant	the elephant
dair ellayfunt	
das Schwein	the pig
dass shvine	

One animal on the word list isn't anyone's favourite. Can you spot which one it is?

Du bist dran

Tell someone in German which colour you like best. Try saying what your favourite animal is. You can use what Katja's friends are saying to help you.

Warum sind
vahroom zint
Elefanten groß
ellayfunten grawss
und grau?
oont graow

Wenn sie klein
venn zee klyne
und weiß wären, dann
oont vice vairen dun
würden sie Schneeflocken
verden zee shnayflocken
sein.
zyne

Meine
Lieblingsfarbe
ist grün. Mein
Lieblingstier ist
die Katze.

Meine
Lieblingsfarbe
ist rot. Mein
Lieblingstier ist
der Hund.

Meine
Lieblingsfarbe
ist blau. Mein
Lieblingstier ist
das Schwein.

Colour guide

blau
blaow
rot
rawt
grün
grewn
orange
oronsh
gelb
gelp
lila
leelah
weiß
vice
schwarz
shvahrts
braun
brown

In German, colour words
and other describing words
(adjectives) often change their
spelling and sound when they
are used in different parts of
sentences. On this page, they
are all the same as on
the guide.

15

Joke: Why are elephants big and grey?
If they were small and white, then they'd be snowflakes.

German calendar

Silvia and her friends are making German calendars which last for twelve years. You can make one too by following the instructions below.

You will need:
2 sheets of cardboard about 29cm by 21cm (11in by 8in), scissors, pencils and felt tip pens, a ruler and some glue.

Use the word list to find out the names of the months in German. Look back at page 10 if you can't remember which day of the week is which.

1. Use the ruler to draw 3cm (1in) squares over one of the sheets of cardboard, then cut the sheet into strips lengthwise (each strip 3cm (1in) wide).

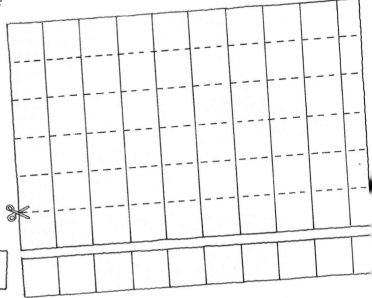

2. Each strip will have just over nine squares on it. On the first strip, leave one full blank square at either end, then write in the days of the week in German, one on each square, like this:

3. Stick the next two strips together to make one very long strip and mark numbers 1-16 on one side, again leaving a blank square at either end. Don't cut these off. Draw 3cm (1in) squares on the other side and write in numbers 17-31.

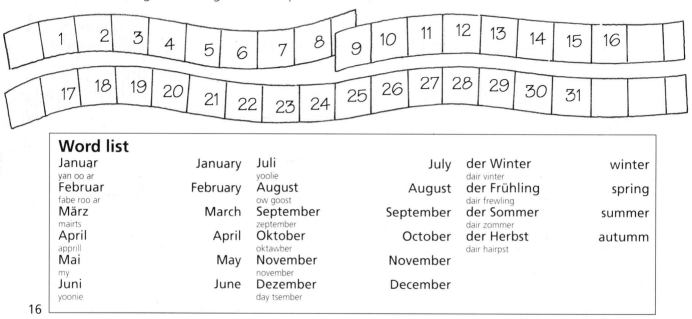

Word list

Januar *yan oo ar*	January	Juli *yoolie*	July	der Winter *dair vinter*	winter
Februar *fabe roo ar*	February	August *ow goost*	August	der Frühling *dair frewling*	spring
März *mairts*	March	September *zeptember*	September	der Sommer *dair zommer*	summer
April *apprill*	April	Oktober *oktawber*	October	der Herbst *dair hairpst*	autumm
Mai *my*	May	November *november*	November		
Juni *yoonie*	June	Dezember *day tsember*	December		

4. On the next strip write the months in German: *Januar* to *Juni* on one side and *Juli* to *Dezember* on the other. This time you will have more than one square left over. Don't cut them off as you will need them to pull the strips through the calendar.

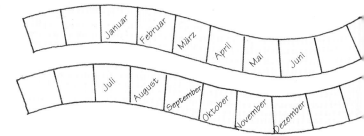

5. The last strip is for the years. Write 1993 to 1998 on one side and 1999 to 2004 on the other.

6. Mark off the second sheet as shown below:

Cut slots along the lines. Thread your strips through to show the right day, date, month and year.

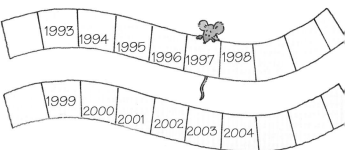

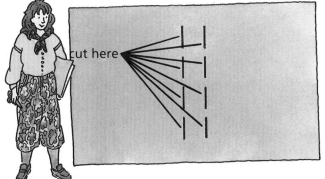

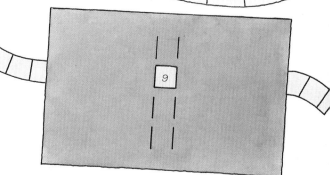

Silvia and the others are decorating an enormous calendar they have made for the classroom. You could decorate the front of your calendar too, using the different seasons.

Wie nennt man
vee nennt mun
ein Baby, das im Juni
ine baby dass im yoonie
geboren wird?
gebawren veert

Junior
yoonie or

Joke: What do you call a baby born in June? Junior.

What is it?

Frau Ziffer has divided the class into teams to play a guessing game. The teams wear blindfolds and take turns to pick objects out of a large box. They must guess what they have picked out.

To ask what something is in German, you say *ist es...?* [ist ess], which means "is it...?" and then the name of the object.

To answer, you say *ja, es ist...* [yah ess ist], which means "yes, it's...", or *nein, es ist...* [nine ess ist], which means "no, it's...".

Using the word list to help you, can you answer everyone's questions?

Du bist dran
Point out to a friend something you know the name of in German and say *ist es...?* [ist ess] followed by a different name. Your friend must try and tell you the correct name, using *nein, es ist...* [nine ess ist].

Word list

ist es...?	ist ess	is it...?
ja	yah	yes
nein	nine	no
es ist	ess ist	it is
eine Blockflöte	ine a blockflerta	a recorder
ein Lutscher	ine lootcher	a lollipop
ein Buch	ine bookh	a book
ein Portemonnaie	ine port monnay	a purse
ein Drachen	ine drakhen	a kite
eine Muschel	ine a mooshel	a shell
eine Pfeife	ine a pfyfa	a whistle
ein Schläger	ine shlayger	a racket
eine Armbanduhr	ine a armband oor	a wristwatch
ein Bleistift	ine bly shtift	a pencil

18

Song

Here is a song to sing in German. Can you guess what any of the words mean? You can check what they all mean on page 32.

Was ist das da? Was seh' ich? Es ist wirk-lich wun-der-lich.
vass ist dass dah vass zay ikh ess ist veerk likh voon der likh

Es ist kein ver-rück-tes Schwein, kann auch kein-e Schlan-ge sein.
ess ist kine fair rook tess shvine kann owkh kine a shlun ga zine

Was ist das da? Was seh' ich? Mei-ne Kat-ze. Sie liebt mich!
vass ist dass dah vass zay ikh my na kat sa zee leept mikh

Ist es ein Drachen?

Ist es eine Muschel?

Was hat acht
vass hat akht
Beine, zwei Räder
byna, tsvy raider
und fährt schnell?
oont fairt shnell

Eine Spinne auf
ine a shpinna owf
einem Motorrad.
ine um motawr raht

Ist es ein Drachen?

Ist es eine Pfeife?

Joke: What has eight legs, two wheels and goes fast?
A spider on a motorbike.

Hide and seek

Katja and Markus are playing hide and seek. It's Markus's turn to hide. Can you spot him? (If you can't remember who Markus is, look back to page 5.)

To say, "There he is," in German you say *Da ist er* [dah ist air].

Wo ist Katja? [vaw ist katya]. Where is Katja? To say, "There she is," you say *Da ist sie* [dah ist zee].

Which paths must Katja take to reach Markus by the shortest route? She cannot use any of the paths which are blocked by children or objects.

Word list

wo ist vaw ist	where is
da ist er dah ist air	there he, it is
da ist sie dah ist zee	there she, it is
da ist es dah ist ess	there it is
die Katze dee katsa	cat
das Fahrrad dass fahrraht	bicycle
der Drachen dair drukhen	kite
die Fahne dee fahna	flag
der Gärtner dair gairtner	gardener

Can you spot some other things in the picture? Say *Da ist er* [dah ist air] when you spot a *der* word, *Da ist sie* [dah ist zee] for a *die* word and *Da ist es* [dah ist ess] for a *das* word.

Wo ist der Drachen?

Wo ist die Katze?

Wo ist das Fahrrad?

20 Wo ist die Fahne?

Joke: What goes clip-clop, clip thud?
A horse with a wooden leg.

Tongue twister

How fast can you say this tongue twister without making any mistakes?

Fischers Fritz fischt
fishers frits fisht
frische Fische. Frische Fische
frisha fisha frisha fisha
fischt Fischers Fritz.
fisht fishers frits

21

Here is what it means in English: *The Fischers' Fritz fishes fresh fish. Fresh fish is what the Fischers' Fritz fishes.*

Sports day

Today is sports day. Frau Ziffer is asking who knows how to climb, *Wer kann klettern?* [vair kan klettern]. Silvia answers, *Ich kann klettern* [ikh kan klettern] which means, "I know how to climb".

Use the word list to help you answer these questions for the people in the picture. Point to someone who is doing each activity and say *ich kann* [ikh kan] for them and then what he or she is doing.

Wer kann Handstand machen?
Wer kann laufen?
Wer kann kriechen?
Wer kann einen Purzelbaum machen?
Wer kann ein Rad schlagen?
Wer kann hüpfen?
Wer kann springen?

Wer kann klettern?

Ich kann klettern.

Herr Doktor, der
hair doctawr dair
unsichtbare Mensch
oonzikhtbara mensh
wartet auf Sie.
vahrtet owf zee

Sagen Sie ihm,
zahgen zee eem
ich kann ihn
ikh kan een
nicht sehen.
nikht zayen

Du bist dran
Do you know how to do any of the things in the picture? Look at the word list to see how to say what you can do in German. Remember, say *ich kann* [ikh kan] and then what you can do.

Joke: Doctor, the invisible man's waiting for you. Tell him I can't see him.

22

Word list

German	Pronunciation	English
wer kann...?	vair kan	who can...?
ich kann	ikh kan	I can
kannst du...?	kanst doo	can you...?
laufen	laowfen	to run
Handstand machen	huntshtunt makhen	to do a handstand
ein Rad schlagen	ine raht shlahgn	to do a cartwheel
einen Purzelbaum machen	ine n poortselbaowm makhen	to do a somersault
hüpfen	hoopfen	to hop
kriechen	kreekhen	to crawl
klettern	klettern	to climb
springen	shpringen	to jump

German flip-flaps

Here is how to make and use a German flip-flap.

You will need:

a large square of paper and some felt tips.

Fold each corner of your paper square into the middle. Turn the paper over and do the same on the other side.

Write numbers 2 to 9, one on each of the small triangles you can now see.

Lift up the four flaps in turn. Under each number, write down *kannst du* [kanst doo], which means "can you" followed by one of the activites from the word list. You will have to write in little writing to fit in all the words.

Fold the flaps in again and turn the square back over.

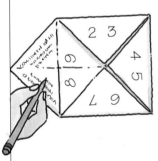

Write *blau, rot, grün* and *gelb* on the four small squares. Fill them in with your felt tips. (Look back at page 14 if you can't remember which ones to use).

Slide both your index fingers and thumbs under the squares and push them together like this:

Ask a friend to choose a square. Say the word on it, then do this as you spell it out:

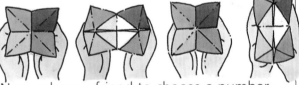

Now ask your friend to choose a number. Count it out in German, opening your flip-flap to the top and side as before. (If you can't remember all the numbers in German, look back at page 8.)

When you finish counting, ask your friend to choose another number. This time, open up that flap and read out loud in German what it says under the number your friend has chosen. Your friend must do the activity you read, or start again.

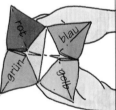

Lunchtime

Today, lunch is outside. Unfortunately, not everyone seems to be having a good time.

Birgit [beer git] is in a bad mood because she has ripped her skirt. *Ich bin schlecht gelaunt* [ikh bin shlekht gelaownt] means, "I am in a bad mood," in German.

How do you think the other children are feeling? Use the word list to help you match each speech bubble below with a child in the picture. Can you say each one out loud in German?

Mir ist heiß.

Mir ist kalt.

Ich habe Hunger.

Ich habe Durst.

Ich habe Durst.

Ich habe Hunger.

Ich bin glücklich.

Ich bin müde.

Ich bin traurig.

Ich habe Hunger.

Du bist dran

How do you feel at the moment?

Use the word list to describe how you feel in German. Say it out loud.

24

Ich bin schlecht gelaunt.

Nenne mir
nenna meer
dreißig Tiere, die
dryssikh teera dee
aus Afrika kommen.
owss afree kah kommen

Neunundzwanzig
noyn oont tsvantsikh
Elefanten und eine
ellayfunten oont ine a
Giraffe.
gear affa

Joke: Name 30 animals which come from Africa.
29 elephants and a giraffe.

Word list

In German, describing words (adjectives) often change their sound and spelling. This depends on whether they describe *der* words (masculine), *die* words (feminine) or *das* words (neuter) and where they come in a sentence. On this page, all the adjectives stay the same.

ich habe Hunger		I'm hungry
ikh hahba hoonger		
ich habe Durst		I'm thirsty
ikh hahba doorst		
mir ist heiß		I'm hot
meer ist hyss		
mir ist kalt		I'm cold
meer ist kalt		
ich bin		I am
ikh bin		

glücklich		happy
glooklikh		
traurig		sad
traowrikh		
müde		tired
mooda		
schlecht gelaunt		in a bad mood
shlekht gelaownt		

25

Telling the time

Karin must meet Silvia and Katja from school today but her watch is broken so she has to keep asking the time.

To ask the time in German, you say *Wie spät ist es?* [vee shpate ist ess]. To answer, you say *es ist* [ess ist] which means "it is" and then the time.

Uhr [oor] after a number on the clock means "o'clock".

So to say, "It's ten o'clock," in German, you say *Es ist zehn Uhr* [ess ist tsain oor]. How do you say, "It's six o'clock"?

Can you say *Es ist... Uhr* for each of the hours on Oma Strudel's alarm clock?

Now can you spot what time it is in each of these pictures? Answer Karin's question in each one by saying the time out loud in German. Use Oma Strudel's alarm clock to help you with the numbers.

You don't say *halb* with *Mitternacht* or *Mittag*. You say *halb zwölf* [hulp tsverlf].

"One o'clock" is *ein Uhr*, but "one" on its own is *eins* [ine ts]. To say "half past twelve", you say *halb eins* [hulp ine ts].

zwölf Uhr
tsverlf oor

elf Uhr
elf oor

zehn Uhr
tsain oor

neun Uhr
noynoor

acht Uhr
akht oor

sieben Uhr
zeebn oor

sechs Uhr
zex oor

ein Uhr
ine oor

zwei Uhr
tsvy oor

drei Uhr
dry oor

vier Uhr
feer oor

fünf Uhr
foonf oor

Es ist acht Uhr.

Wie spät ist es?

Word list

wie spät ist es? vee shpate ist ess	what time is it?
es ist ... Uhr ess ist ...oor	it's...o'clock
Mittag mittahg	midday
Mitternacht mitternahkht	midnight
halb...* hulp	half ...

*In German, instead of saying "half past", you say "half to" the next hour. So to say "half past one", you say *es ist halb zwei* [ess ist hulp tsvy].

26   A

B

E

Du bist dran

Wie spät ist es? [vee shpate ist ess].
Can you say in German what time it is at the moment? Say it to the nearest half hour. In German, you say "half to" the next hour instead of "half-past". So if you want to say "half-past" you say *halb* [hulp] and then the hour after the one you mean. To say "half past four", you would say *halb fünf* [hulp foonf].

True or false?

Katja and Silvia are playing a game on the way home from school. One of them says something and the other has to say whether it is true or false.

To say, "That's true," in German, say *Das ist richtig* [dass ist rikhtikh]. To say, "That's false," say *Das ist falsch* [dass ist fulsh].

Can you say what the reply to each of their speech bubbles should be? Say the answers out loud. If you don't know, say *Ich weiß es nicht* [ikh vice ess nikht] which means, "I don't know".

Look back through the book if you can't remember any of the words.

Word list

What's the right word?

Frau Ziffer stays late at school to correct everyone's work. Can you help her? Say out loud in German what should be written under each picture.

Das ist [dass ist] means "this is" or "that is". Look back through the book if you can't remember any of the words you need.

Mein Buch ist blau.

Es gibt drei Drachen.

Mein Bruder heißt Oma Strudel.

A — Das ist ein Schwein.

B — Das ist ein Regenschirm.

Das ist eine Muschel.

C — Das ist eine Armbanduhr.

E — Das ist meine Mutter.

Du bist dran

You could make your own picture book in German. Draw something and write what it is in German, using *das ist* [dass ist] and then the name of the object. Remember to check if it is a *der*, *die* or *das* object, so that you know to write *ein* (for *der* and *das* words) or *eine* (for *die* words) before it.

29

Word list

Here is a list of all the German words and phrases** used in this book in alphabetical order. You can use the list either to check quickly what a word means or to test yourself. Cover up any German or English word or phrase and see if you can say its translation. Remember that most words change slightly when you are talking about more than one thing (plural).

acht	akht	eight
achtzehn	akht tsain	eighteen
April	apprill	April
Arm (der)	arm	arm
Armbanduhr (die)	armbandoor	watch
August	ow goost*	August
Bein (das)	bine	leg
blau	blaow	blue
Bleistift (der),	blyshtift	pencil
Bleistifte (die)	blyshtifta	pencils
Blockflöte (die)	blokflerta	recorder
braun	brown	brown
Brille (die)	brilla	glasses
Bruder (der)	brooder	brother
Buch (das),	bookh	book
Bücher (die)	boosher	books
da ist er	dah ist air	there he, it is
da ist es	dah ist es	there it is
da ist sie	dah ist zee	there she, it is
danke	dunka	thank you
das ist	dass ist	this is, that is
der, die, das	dair, dee, dass	the
Deutsch	doytch	German
Dezember	day tsember	December
Dienstag (der)	deenstahg	Tuesday
Donnerstag (der)	donnerstahg	Thursday
Drachen (der)	drakhen	kite
drei	dry	three
dreizehn	dry tsain	thirteen
du bist dran	doo bist dran	your turn
ein, eine	ine, ine a	one, a
ein Rad schlagen	ine raht shlahgn	to do a cartwheel
einen Purzelbaum	ine npoortselbaowm	to do a
machen	makhen	somersault
eins	ine ts	one
Elefant (der)	ellayfunt	elephant
elf	elf	eleven
Englisch	eng glish	English
Entschuldigung	entshooldigoong	sorry

er heißt	air hyste	he is called
(es geht mir)	ess gate meer	I'm very well
sehr gut	zair goot	
es gibt	ess gipt	there is, there are
es ist	ess ist	it is
es ist ... Uhr	ess ist oor	it is ... o'clock
Etui (das)	aytoo ee	pencil case
Fahne (die)	fahna	flag
Fahrrad (das)	fahrraht	bicycle
falsch	fulsh	false
Februar	fabe roo ar	February
Filzstift (der),	filts shtift	felt tip pen
Filzstifte (die)	filts shtifta	felt tip pens
Frau (die)	fraow	Mrs. , woman
Freitag (der)	frytahg	Friday
Frühling (der)	frewling	spring
fünf	foonf*	five
fünfzehn	foonf* tsain	fifteen
Fuß	fooss	foot
Gärtner (der)	gairtner	gardener
gelb	gelp	yellow
Geschenk (das),	geshenk	present
Geschenke (die)	geshenka	presents
glücklich	glooklikh*	happy
grün	grewn	green
Gürtel (der)	girtle	belt
Guten Tag	gootn tahg	hello
halb	hulp	half
Hallo	hullaw	hi
Hand (die)	hunt	hand
Handschuh (der),	hunt shoo	glove
Handschuhe (die)	hunt shooa	gloves
Handstand	huntshtunt	to do a
machen	makhen	handstand
Heft (das)	heft	exercise book
Herbst (der)	hairpst	autumn
Herr	hair	Mr.
heute	hoyta	today
Himmel-und-Hölle	himmel oont* herla	hopscotch
Hund (der)	hoont*	dog
hüpfen	hoopfen*	to hop
Hut (der),	hoot,	hat,
Hüte (die)	hoota	hats
ich bin	ikh bin	I am
ich habe ...	ikh hahba	I have lost
verloren	fairlawren	
ich habe	ikh hahba	I have a
Bauchweh	baowkhvay	tummy-ache
ich habe Durst	ikh hahba doorst	I'm thirsty

30

*The "oo" sound in these words is like the "u" in "put".
**Except those in the jokes and songs, which are translated on the pages or on the answer page.

ich habe Hunger	ikh hahbahoonger*	I'm hungry
ich habe Kopfweh	ikh hahba kopfvay	I have a headache
ich habe Zahnweh	ikh hahba tsahnvay	I have toothache
ich heiße	ikh hyssa	I am called
ich kann	ikh kan	I can
ich weiß es nicht	ikh vice ess nikht	I don't know
ist es...?	ist ess...?	is it...?
ja	yah	yes
Januar	yan oo ar	January
Juli	yoolie	July
Juni	yoonie	June
kannst du ...?	kanst doo	can you...?
Katze (die)	katsa	cat
klettern	klettern	to climb
kriechen	kreekhen	to crawl
laufen	laowfen	to run
lila	leelah	purple
Lutscher (der)	lootcher*	lollipop
Mai	my	May
März	mairts	March
Maus (die)	mouse	mouse
mein Bein tut mir weh	mine bine toot meer vay	my leg hurts
mein Lieblingstier ist...	mine leeblingsteer ist	my favourite animal is...
mein, meine, meinen	mine, myna, mynen	my
meine Lieblingsfarbe ist...	myna leeblingsfarba ist	my favourite colour is...
mir ist heiß	meer ist hyss	I'm hot
mir ist kalt	meer ist kalt	I'm cold
Mittag	mittahg	midday
Mitternacht	mitternahkht	midnight
Mittwoch (der)	mitvokh	Wednesday
Montag (der)	mawntahg	Monday
müde	mooda	tired
Muschel (die)	mooshel*	shell
Musik	moozeek	music
Mutter (die)	mootter*	mother
nein	nine	no
neun	noyn	nine
neunzehn	noyn tsain	nineteen
November	november	November
Oktober	oktawber	October
Oma (die)	awma	Granny
Onkel (der)	onkel	uncle
orange	oronsh	orange
Pfeife (die)	pfyffa	whistle
Pferd (das)	pfairt	horse
Pflanze (die), Pflanzen (die)	pfluntsa pfluntsen	plant plants
Portemonnaie (das)	port monnay	purse
Regenschirm (der), Regenschirme (die)	raygn sheerm raygn sheerma	umbrella umbrellas
richtig	rikhtikh	true
rot	rawt	red
Samstag (der)	zamstahg	Saturday
Schläger (der)	shlayger	racket
schlecht gelaunt	shlekht gelaownt	in a bad mood
schwarz	shvahrts	black
Schwein (das)	shvine	pig
Schwester (die)	shvester	sister
sechs	zex	six
sechzehn	zekh tsain	sixteen
September	zeptember	September
sie heißt	zee hyste	she is called
sieben	zeebn	seven
siebzehn	zeep tsain	seventeen
Sommer (der)	zommer	summer
Sonntag (der)	zonntahg	Sunday
Sport	shport	sport
springen	shpringen	to jump
Strickjacke (die)	shtrik yukka	cardigan
traurig	traowrikh	sad
und	oont*	and
Vater (der)	fahter	father
vier	feer	four
vierzehn	feer tsain	fourteen
weiß	vice	white
wer kann ... ?	vair kan	who can...?
wie geht's?	vee gates	how are you?
wie heißt du?	vee hyste doo	what's your name?
wie spät ist es?	vee shpate ist ess	what's the time?
Winter (der)	vinter	winter
wo ist...?	vaw ist	where is...?
Wochenende (das)	vokhen enda	week-end
zehn	tsain	ten
Zeichnen	tsykhnen	drawing, art
zwanzig	tsvan tsikh	twenty
zwei	tsvy	two
zwölf	tsverlf	twelve

Answers

PAGE 4-5
This is the way Jörg should go:

Here are the German answers to the questions:
Sie heißt Silvia. *Er heißt Herr Strudel.*

PAGE 6-7
Frau Strudel should say, *Mein Bein tut mir weh.*
Oma Strudel should say, *Es geht mir sehr gut.*
Herr Strudel should say, *Ich habe Kopfweh.*
Rainer should say, *Ich habe Bauchweh.*

PAGE 8-9
Es gibt acht Pflanzen. *Es gibt fünf Geschenke.*
Es gibt drei *Es gibt neun Bleistifte.*
 Regenschirme. *Es gibt sieben Hüte.*

Here is the tune for the song:

```
1. Ein Hund woll - te    spiel'n,    woll - te Fuß - ball spiel - en,
   ine hoont voll  ta    shpeeln     voll   ta fooss bal  shpeel en

   Ein Hund und sein Herr   woll - ten Fuß - ball  spiel - en.
   ine hoont oont zine hair  voll  ten fooss bal   shpeel en

2. Zwei Hund' woll - ten   spiel'n,   woll - ten Fuß - ball  spiel - en,
   tsvy hoont  voll  ten   shpeeln    voll   ten fooss bal   shpeel en

   Zwei Hund', ein Hund und sein Herr  woll - ten Fuß - ball spiel - en.
   tsvy hoont ine hoont oont zine hair  voll  ten fooss bal  shpeel en

3. Drei Hund' woll - ten   spiel'n,   woll - ten Fuß - ball  spiel - en,
   dry hoont  voll  ten    shpeeln    voll   ten fooss bal   shpeel en

   Drei Hund', zwei Hund', ein Hund und sein Herr  woll - ten Fuß - ball spiel - en.
   dry hoont tsvy hoont ine hoont oont zine hair   voll  ten fooss bal shpeel en
```

PAGE 10-11
A. *Es ist Montag.* C. *Es ist Freitag.*
B. *Es ist Donnerstag.* D. *Es ist Dienstag.*

PAGE 14-15

Der Elefant (the elephant) isn't anyone's favourite.

PAGE 18-19
This is what the words mean in English:
> What is that there? What do I see?
> It is really heavenly.
> It is not a mad pig,
> Nor can it be a snake,
> What is that there? What do I see?
> My cat. She loves me.

PAGE 20-21
This is the way Katja should go:

PAGE 26-27
A. *Es ist neun Uhr.* D. *Es ist drei Uhr.*
B. *Es ist elf Uhr.* E. *Es ist vier Uhr.*
C. *Es ist ein Uhr.*

PAGE 28-29
A. *Das ist falsch.* D. *Das ist richtig.*
B. *Das ist richtig.* E. *Das ist falsch.*
C. *Das ist falsch.* F. *Das ist falsch.*

Here is what should be written under each picture:

A. *Das ist ein Hund.* D. *Das ist ein Bleistift.*
B. *Das ist ein Buch.* E. *Das ist mein Vater.*
C. *Das ist ein Hut.*